Fog Hounds Wind Cat Sea Mice

JOAN AIKEN

Illustrated by Peter Bailey

Hodder
Children's
Books

a division of Hodder Headline plc

Printed and bound in Great Britain by
Mackays of Chatham PLC, Chatham, Kent

Hodder Children's Books
A Division of Hodder Headline plc
338 Euston Road
London NW1 3BH

CONTENTS

FOG HOUNDS

A BOY CALLED TAD WAS painting the front door of the house where he and his sister lived, one mild September evening. Using fast-drying paint, he was painting the door a beautiful honeysuckle yellow, and he had nearly finished the job, which was just as well, for dusk was beginning to wrap the village in shadows. Very few people were about, and lights were twinkling out, one by one, in the cottage windows.

The boy's sister, Ermina, rattled the curtains apart and put her head out of the front window.

'Tad? Haven't you finished yet?' she called. 'Make haste, it's nearly Hound Time.'

In the country where Tad and

Ermina lived, it was dangerous to be
out of doors after sunset. The reason for
this was the tribe of huge misty
creatures, known as the Fog Hounds,
which roamed all over the land from
dusk to dawn; they went ranging and
loping through towns and villages, past
factories and farms, through fields and
forests. Their feet made no noise on the
ground, they were pale grey and half
transparent, like smoke, so that you
could see lamp-posts and letter-boxes
through them and beyond them. Most
of the time they ran along silently, with
their noses down close to the ground,
but every now and then one of them
would lift his head and howl, and when
he did, what a bloodcurdling sound *that*
was! It almost made the blood run
backwards in your veins.

Nobody who had been chased by the Fog Hounds ever came back alive to tell the tale of what had happened to him. The hounds belonged to the King, and were supposed to chase only criminals and wrongdoers. But the King was old, very old and sick, and had lost most of his  wits; it was said that he didn't care what the hounds did any more.

So Ermina called anxiously: 'Tad! Come along! Leave the door if you haven't finished, it must wait till the morning. Come inside!'

Ermina was fifteen years older than her brother; and she was a Wise Woman, which is halfway to being a witch. She possessed a pack of cards which could fly, like a flight of swallows, from one of her hands to the other; and she could read people's futures in tea-leaves or apple-peelings or duck-feathers.

She made a living by advising people, and telling them what to do if they were unable to make up their minds. The only future she could not read was that of Tad, her own younger brother. When she looked at the cards or the tea-leaves they told her nothing about him; and that was why she worried whenever she thought he might be taking a risk.

'It's all right, Minnie,' Tad called back now. 'I'm just putting on the last lick of paint.'

He did so, admired his work, and was about to open the door and step inside the house, when he heard hasty, running footsteps, and a voice that called frantically, 'Stop, stop! Wait! Help me, please help me!'

Tad waited, with the paint-pot in one hand, and the brush in the other, and he saw a man running at full speed along the village street. A very queer-looking man he was - Tad had never seen anything like him before. On one side of his head the hair was black; on the other side it was white. One of his eyes was blue, the other was brown. One of his hands was black, the other was white; and his jacket and trousers were divided down the middle, red on the left, black on the right.

He was dusty and muddy and his clothes were ragged, and he ran with a stumble and a limp. Sweat poured down his cheeks and he seemed ready to fall to the ground from weariness, yet he was running at a desperate speed and kept looking back over his shoulder in terror.

'They're after me!' he panted.

'Who are?' said Tad, though he guessed.

'The King's soldiers. The Fog Hounds. Save me, oh, save me!'

Then Tad noticed that in the man's left hand – which was the black one – he clutched a golden sprig – it had a flower and leaves and roots; it seemed to be alive, yet it seemed to be made of pure gold.

At this moment, in the distance Tad thought he could hear a sound of sirens wailing, horns blowing, hounds giving tongue, and the clatter of hoofs.

The front window flew open again and Ermina put her head out a second time.

'*Tad!* Make haste and come inside!'

Then she saw the stranger on the footway and said sharply, 'Why are you keeping my brother out of the house? Don't you know it is dangerous? It is almost Hound Time. Who are you?'

'My name is Doubleman,' said the stranger. 'The King's soldiers are after me. I beseech you to save me!'

'Why are they after you? What did you do wrong? Why should we save you? If we take you in, we shall be in danger too,' argued Ermina.

Now the sound of galloping hoofs and wailing sirens could be heard much closer; and also the dreadful throaty pealing bay of the Fog Hounds.

'I helped myself to a golden sprig from the Royal Mint,' said the stranger. 'The hounds have scented it; that is why they are after me.'

'Throw it away, then,' said Ermina. 'What right had you to take it?'

'Throw it away?' panted the man. 'After I have gone to so much trouble to steal it? Never!'

His breath streamed out of his mouth in a white cloud, like the smoke from acid. Tad noticed that a rose growing by their gate began to wither, where the stranger had breathed on its leaves and flowers; they turned black, and shrank together, and fell from their stalks.

The man coughed several times and drew in deep, hacking breaths. Then he pulled a cigarette from his pocket, blew on the tip until it glowed scarlet, put it into his mouth, and sucked heavily on it.

'Tad! Come inside!' Ermina cried shrilly. 'It's mad to stay out there. We can't help you at all,' she told the stranger. 'If you robbed the Royal Mint, then you must look out for yourself.'

'Could you keep the golden sprig for me? If it's not on me, perhaps the hounds won't catch me—'

'And have them catch us instead?
Not likely!' said Ermina, and she flung
open the front door, dragged Tad
inside, and then slammed the door and
bolted it.

The stranger called Doubleman glanced hastily up and down the street, dragging hard on his cigarette as he did so, until the tip glowed gold. Then he ran on a few yards, and tossed the golden sprig into a builders' rubbish skip which stood a short way along the road, outside an empty house. Leaving the sprig there, Doubleman ran on, going faster and more easily after his short rest; soon he had vanished into the dusk.

Tad, who had looked out through the open window, saw what Doubleman did, but he did not tell Ermina, who was angrily bustling about, slapping plates and mugs on the table for their evening meal.

Tad hoped very much that Doubleman would escape from the King's soldiers, for he could imagine how dreadful it must be to be hunted.

Ermina, however, felt differently.

'Did you see what happened to our white rose when he breathed on it?' she said. 'Did you see how he lit his cigarette by blowing on the tip? That man belongs to darkness, let darkness take him! He is a bad soul. I am sorry that he even stood outside our gate. And if he stole that sprig from the Royal Mint, he certainly deserves to be caught and punished.'

Very soon the King's soldiers came thundering along the village street astride their grey horses, with muskets cocked, and blue lights burning on the horses' brow-bands, and sirens wailing and warbling, and horns blaring.

Ahead of the horses ran the Fog Hounds, paler than vapour and silent as smoke. They flowed over the cobbles of the street as smoothly as mist; but their eyes now and then glittered like red pennies. And from time to time one of them, catching the scent of the man they were after, would raise his muzzle and let out a long howl.

When they reached the cottage of Tad and Ermina, the hounds paused for a moment, sniffing a patch of ground where Doubleman had stood, snuffling at the blackened rose petals which had fallen to the ground when he breathed on them.

Trembling, watching through the crack between the curtains, Tad could see their grey, smoky heads weave this way and that, questing low down over the scent. They pawed, with their big soundless transparent feet, at the cigarette ash that lay by the gatepost; then, noses close to the fresh trail, they went drifting on down the street until they came to the builders' rubbish skip into which Doubleman had thrown his golden sprig. There they checked again, whimpering and snarling, chopping to and fro in the road like a pulse of grey cloud that divides round a crag.

Tad could not help a shudder as he watched the snakelike motion of their necks and shadowy muzzles. And yet there was something beautiful about them too; he loved the careless way in which they flowed over the ground, smoothly as the wind itself. If only they were not in pursuit of that wretched man! If only they were not used to hunt down criminals!

If I were King, thought Tad, I would use my fog hounds in a different way, so that people need not be afraid of them.

Soon the Fog Hounds left the builders' container, and drifted on along the street, seeming to go quite slowly, yet the soldiers on their swift grey horses had to gallop to keep up with them.

They vanished much too soon for Tad, who hung out of the window to see the last of them, blue lights gleaming and sirens screaming as they careered out of sight.

'Shut the window, Tad, and draw the curtains,' urged Ermina.

'I wonder if the man will get away?' he said.

'If that man robbed the King's mint, he deserves to be caught. Here, put this teapot on the table, and the dish of apples.'

'I'd love to have a Fog Hound of my own,' said Tad, taking the teapot, which was red and gold, shaped and glazed like a crown.

'Are you *mad*? The Fog Hounds belong to the King,' said Ermina, taking a big brown loaf from the oven. 'Cut the bread and stop talking nonsense.'

Tad cut the loaf of bread, and took an apple from the dish. But as he munched his crisp crust, and crunched his juicy apple, he remembered that one

of the Fog Hounds, smaller than the
rest, no more than a puppy, had run
behind the pack, with its smoky tail
blowing out behind it like a tail of
cirrus cloud. I wish that puppy
belonged to me, he thought longingly.
And when they had finished supper and
were sitting with elbows on the table-
cloth among crumbs and empty teacups
and plates covered with apple-peel, Tad
said, 'Tell my fortune, Min!'

'What's the use?' said she crossly.
'You know it never works. The cards
won't answer. They turn their faces
away and sulk.'

She picked up the pack of cards
and tossed them, so that they flew like
swallows from her left hand to her
right, and then rippled out on to the
table in a semi-circle. Sure enough,

although she had tossed them with faces upturned, they fell face down; but Tad thought he had caught a glimpse of the King of Diamonds, and he thought the King had given him a wink as he fell. 'Try the tea-leaves then, Min,' said Tad.

Ermina took his empty cup, turned it over, and tapped it three times. Then she turned it right way up again. Inside the cup, the tea-leaves had formed a perfect ring, around the rim.

'They never did *that* before,' said she, staring. 'What can it mean?'

She gave her brother a worried look.

'You're the Wise Woman, Min, you should know.'

'Well I don't know,' she snapped. 'There's only one thing – but no, that's impossible. It must be an accident.' And she frowned, biting her lip.

'Try it again.'

'You must never try more than once. *You* know that.'

'Try the apple peel, then.'

'Throw it up.'

Tad tossed up the unbroken rind of the apple he had been eating (which was a Ribstone Pippin). His elbow caught against the arm of his chair, the peel flew into the fire, and nothing came out but a long curl of hissing smoke, like a tail of cirrus cloud.

'It's no use,' said Ermina. 'Nothing answers. And it's time for bed.'

Tad lit his candle, and prepared to go up to his attic room.

'Min,' he asked, standing on the bottom stair, 'who do you really think that Doubleman was?'

'He was a wrong one,' said Ermina. 'Remember how he lit that cigarette by blowing on it? And he wasn't a bit ashamed of having robbed the King's Mint. I expect the soldiers will have caught him by now.'

But Tad, as he lay in bed, thought: Perhaps Doubleman was not all bad. And he did leave the golden sprig behind. Perhaps he will manage to escape. I hope so. If he can run as far as the Black Mire, he may get away.

The Black Mire was a wide and deep marsh which lay three miles westward of the village. There was no path across it.

Later that night Tad woke, and heard the King's soldiers returning slowly, at a walking pace. Slipping out of bed, Tad put his eye to a crack between two roof tiles, and so was able to look down into the street. By bright moonlight he could see the soldiers, riding slowly on tired horses, and the hounds following slowly behind like the plume of smoke that follows a steamship. But he could see no prisoner.

Next day it was whispered in the village that the man had escaped the soldiers and run into the Black Mire; he must have sunk into the bog and drowned there.

Tad took his paint pots and went to paint the doors and windows of a house at the end of the village. On his way past, he glanced into the builders' skip. There lay the golden sprig, among dust and broken bricks and rusty nails and splintered wood.

What should I do about it? wondered Tad. It belongs to the King's Mint. I suppose I ought to tell somebody about it, and then it would be taken back.

But, as he stood looking at the golden sprig, a swallow swooped down, snatched up the sprig in its beak, flew to the village green, where there was a round pond, and dropped the sprig into the water. Tad, running after the swallow, was just in time to see the golden leaves gleam as they settled under the clear water, down on the

muddy bottom of the
pond. Swallows are wise
birds, Ermina told her
brother once. They know the secrets of
summer and winter. Always believe
them, always follow them.

I'll leave the golden sprig where
it is, thought Tad. He remembered
another thing his sister had once told
him: If you ever meet a demon, or a
spirit from another world, take great
care not to touch or hold any object
that the demon has touched, for it may
do you terrible harm. Wait forty days
before you touch it, even if it is a rock
that blocks your path.

Perhaps, thought Tad, Doubleman
was such a spirit. I'll wait. The swallow is
a wise bird. Lying in the pond, below the
clean water, that golden sprig can harm

nobody. Let it stay there forty days.

And so Tad went off about his business, painting doors and windows and fences. But every day he walked past the pond on the green. And when he did so, he noticed that the golden sprig was growing. It had sent roots down into the mud, and it was putting out new leaves, sprouting long stalks and thrusting up tendrils towards the surface of the water.

On the fortieth day, one little sprout thick with flower buds broke the surface of the water, and Tad, walking home in the evening sun, saw the buds, and thought: Now, surely it would be safe to pick off just that one stalk. Forty days have passed, and the sprig is ten times the size that it was when Doubleman stole it from the King's

Mint. I shall not be robbing the King if I take one little stalk covered with buds.

He leaned out over the surface of the water, where swallows were swooping and catching flies. He carefully reached out his hand, and he picked the little golden sprig. As soon as he picked it, all the buds opened into round golden flowers like tiny cups. Oh, how beautiful it is! thought Tad, gazing in delight at the golden thing that lay cupped in his hand. The flowers were like six little golden suns in his palm.

He stood there so long, bewitched, gazing at the beautiful thing he held, that the real sun slipped down out of sight, dropping into the west beyond the Black Mire, and long evening shadows slid across the green and turned to grey twilight.

'Best get indoors, Tad, boy!' called one or two villagers, making for their houses. 'Fog Hound time coming! Don't loiter about, now!'

'Thank you,' called Tad, without paying heed to what they said. And still he stood, with his eyes on the golden sprig in his hand, while the light grew dimmer and dimmer and the mist began to rise in white wreaths from the water of the pool, and from the Black Mire in the distance.

Tad's left hand, the hand that did not hold the sprig, hung down by his side, and now, all of a sudden, he felt something touch that hand – something that felt cool, soft, and a little damp. He gave a gasp of surprise and fright, glancing behind him. What thing could have touched his hand so coldly and

softly, feeling like a snowflake? Then he
gasped again, but this time with pure
astonishment. For just behind him stood
a transparent Fog Hound puppy, wagging its misty feathery tail. And what he
had felt must have been the touch of its
tongue. It must have licked his hand. It
looked up at him, wagging its tail again,
and he saw that its eyes were not red,
but pure and burning gold.

'You licked my hand!' whispered Tad. 'Oh, you beautiful Fog Hound – you licked my hand!'

Ranged behind the puppy, as he looked across the darkening green, Tad saw the whole pack of ghostly Fog Hounds. Their heads were raised, ears pricked, tails mistily waving in the dusk; he could see their eyes glisten like luminous glow-worms; he could see their breath rise like the vapour from the pond water.

Without the least fear, Tad walked among the Fog Hounds, and felt them softly brush against him.

They felt cold and soft and airy, as a bubble does when it bursts. They licked his hands. He felt them press against him, cool and feathery as clouds.

Poor, poor Doubleman, thought Tad. If only he had known. If only he had kept the golden sprig, he would have been safe from the hounds. If he had kept the sprig, this would have been happening to *him,* not to me.

But then Tad wondered: Perhaps Doubleman meant to leave the sprig in that builders' skip? Perhaps he meant me to find it? How shall I ever be sure?

At last, at very long last, Tad went back home. He said goodnight to the Fog Hounds; he patted and stroked their cloudy, downy heads, he hugged the Fog Puppy who had first licked his hand; and he opened the door of the house and went in. How shall I ever begin to explain to Ermina what has happened to me? he wondered.

But Ermina, listening to the radio,

had not even noticed how late her brother came home. She was pale and shocked and wide-eyed with news.

'Just listen to this!' she said. 'The King is dead! The old King! He died at the age of a hundred and eighteen! And - only think! - he has left no heir! All his sons died before him, and all their sons too. There is nobody left in direct line.'

'How in the world will they choose the next King then?' asked Tad.

'The Fog Hounds are going to choose,' said Ermina. 'That is what I just heard on the radio. The man that the Fog Hounds recognise, and take as their master, that person will be the next King, whoever it is . . . Why, Tad, where in the world did you get those flowers?'

She had just noticed the sprig of
golden flowers that her brother carried
in his hand. Ever since Tad had picked
the sprig, the flowers had been growing, and now they were as big as roses,
and they seemed to shine and give out
light.

They shone, indeed, as brightly as
the eyes of the Fog Hounds, who lay in
silence outside the cottage, ring upon
ring upon ring of them, keeping guard
over their new King until night was
over, and the sun rose again.

WIND CAT

TWO HOUSES FACED EACH OTHER cornerways over a crossroads: one of them was called Carfax, and the other one Bide-a-Wee. Carfax was very old, long and low, built of stone with a stone roof; Bide-a-Wee was much bigger, and built of bright pink brick, with red tiles, yellow thatch, and coloured glass in the front door. It looked like a house from a picture-book. In pink-and-yellow Bide-a-Wee lived Mr and Mrs Blyde, with their dog Spot and their cat Tib; while in the stone house called Carfax, Lukey Web had just come to live with her Aunt Mildrith.

'Is that your cat, Aunt Mildrith?' asked Lukey, when she first caught sight of striped Tib, crouched in the fork of a walnut tree, watching a pair of black-birds who were watching him.

'No, he's not my cat, he belongs to the Blydes. I don't keep a cat any more,' said Aunt Mildrith, who was thin and grey-eyed, quite young for an aunt, and had dark hair which she wore in a bun. 'Not since old Priam died.'

'Why don't you?' Lukey thought that a house ought to have a cat.

'Well . . . Tib, the Blydes' cat, can come into our garden whenever he wants to, and catch our mice. So that's almost as good. And if an elderly lady living alone keeps a cat, people are bound to say that she is a witch, and that the cat is her Familiar.'

'But you aren't very elderly.'

'You don't have to be very elderly to be a witch.'

'What exactly is a Familiar, Aunt Mildrith?'

'Any animal who helps a witch with her witchery. Mostly a cat or a hedge-hog.'

'You *used* to be a witch, though, didn't you?' Lukey persisted.

'Yes, for a while. But I gave it up.'

Lukey thought this a pity. 'Why did you?'

'Oh,' said her aunt, 'with all these private health insurance schemes, nobody these days needs witches.'

In fact this was not the whole reason. When Lukey's parents died and she came to live at Carfax, Aunt Mildrith had thought it best to give up witchcraft. People are apt to tease you at school if your aunt is a witch, and teachers or parents sometimes complain. So, instead of witchcraft, Aunt Mildrith had begun writing a book on the history of magic mirrors. Besides this she spent a great deal of time studying footprints in the sky through a powerful telescope and taking photographs of them; she had a first-rate collection of pictures.

Mr and Mrs Blyde, who lived in Bide-a-Wee, did not greatly care for their neighbour on the opposite corner of the crossroads. In fact they hardly spoke to Aunt Mildrith, except when they were about to leave on one of their trips to Bournemouth. Mr Blyde was a retired bank manager who collected silver sugar tongs, and his

wife spent her time complaining
because the wooded country around the
crossroads was so very different from
Bournemouth, where Mr Blyde had
managed his bank.

'It's so *quiet* here! And half an hour
to the village, if you walk. And all those
dreary hills and trees wherever you look.
At least in Bournemouth there was
something to see out of the window.'

At least once a month Mr and Mrs
Blyde returned to Bournemouth to
spend a few days at a hotel or visit
friends.

'If only we could afford to go on
living there,' sighed Mrs Blyde. 'But our
house belonged to the bank, you see,
and we had to leave it when Mr B
retired. You can't get a house in
Bournemouth now for less than three
hundred thousand pounds.' She sighed
again. Mrs Blyde was a fat woman with
bright yellow hair, like the thatch on
Bide-a-Wee and eyes the colour of
tinned peas. 'I *like* this house,' she said,

gazing peevishly at Bide-a-Wee, 'I *like* it all right, but just look where it *is*! Your little niece settling in all right, is she, Miss Webb?'

'Yes, thank you,' said Lukey politely. But Mrs Blyde went on, without waiting for an answer, 'Well, then, if you won't mind feeding Tib again while we're away, Miss Webb-' and she handed Aunt Mildrith nine tins of PSalmon and one of dried milk, hurried back to her husband's big fawn-coloured car, shouted 'See you on the twentieth,' jumped in, and slammed the car door.

The Blydes always took their dog Spot with them when they went for a trip to Bournemouth. Spot thoroughly enjoyed a scamper on the sands, Mrs Blyde said. But you can't take a cat to a hotel. Cats prefer to stay at home.

Lukey thought that Tib was a stupid name for the Blydes' cat, who was large and striped and glossy and alert. Aunt Mildrith sometimes addressed him as Carfax, which suited him better. Carfax means 'facing four ways' and the Blydes' cat often seemed able to do that. He was a very watchful cat, and seemed to have eyes at the end of his tail and whiskers. He loved wind, going wild when it blew, dashing like a crazy creature up and down the trunks of trees, in and out of bushes, leaping high into the air, spinning round in a spiral and chasing his tail. At those times he seemed more like a kitten, though Mrs Blyde said he was ten years old – seventy human years. To herself, Lukey thought of him as Wind Cat, and she sometimes called him that when they were out

in the woods together; he often
accompanied her for quite long walks.

'You'd better not spend too much time with him, though,' Aunt Mildrith warned, 'or the Blydes will start saying that he's never at home, and always over with us.'

'Well he never comes indoors,' argued Lukey, and she tossed a ping-pong ball for Carfax, or Wind Cat, who shot after it like a striped rocket.

Very regrettably, the dog Spot, who was growing old and slow and short-sighted, had the misfortune to be run over by a bus in Bournemouth. The Blydes immediately bought a new dog, a big rangy active young Airedale whom they christened Tinker. Tinker was not used to cats, and the first thing he did, on arriving at Bide-a-Wee, was to chase the cat Tib out of the house and up a cherry tree, barking and

scrabbling at the trunk and yelling as
if he had sighted a Tasmanian devil.

'TINKER! *Naughty* boy! *Mustn't*
chase Pussums!' shrieked Mrs Blyde,
but she might as well have spoken to
the doormat.

Nothing would stop Tinker from
chasing the cat, whom he looked on as
his lawful prey. From that day on Tib,
or Carfax, or Wind Cat, spent most of
his days in Aunt Mildrith's garden,
which was protected by a high wall,
whether the Blydes were in Bide-a-Wee
or Bournemouth.

'It's a bit bothering, his spending so
much time here,' sighed Aunt Mildrith.

'You mean we should send him
home to be killed?' said Lukey tearfully.
'Look what that horrible beast has
done!' She was bathing a gash in Wind

Cat's leg where Tinker's razor-sharp teeth had grabbed him just before he leapt to the top of the wall. 'You have got to tell the Blydes to get rid of that awful dog,' Lukey told Aunt Mildrith.

'It really isn't our business. And they may be able to train the dog.'

'Why don't you put a spell on them?'

'Oh, I've given up all that sort of thing,' said Aunt Mildrith hastily. 'I handed over my books and globes and my divining rod to a college of witch-craft.'

'But you can still make weather,' objected Lukey.

'Any beginner can make weather. That's the easiest thing of all.'

It was true that Aunt Mildrith often tossed off a quick shower, when the

garden required watering, or, if the day
was grey and cold, spread a patch of
sunshine on the lawn for Lukey and
Carfax to bask in. When, as sometimes
happened, Mr Blyde noticed this, it
annoyed him very much. He would
glare across the road and mutter,
'Meddling with Nature! Funny sort of
goings on! Shouldn't be allowed, if you

ask *me*!'

Nobody did ask him; perhaps this was what irritated him so much.

The flowers and vegetables in Aunt Mildrith's garden were always three times the size of his, despite the sacks of expensive plant-food and weedkiller and all the complicated garden machines that he kept in his shed.

One day Lukey found Carfax, or Wind Cat, very badly hurt indeed, lying in a clump of thyme in Aunt Mildrith's garden.

This time he had not managed to get away fast enough. Horrified, Lukey ran for her aunt, and together they carried the hurt cat indoors on a strip of matting.

'This calls for powdered vervain and a pinch of mandragora,' muttered Aunt Mildrith, and she fetched out a little muslin bag from the back of a cupboard. From the same place she took out a battered old black book which seemed to have been overlooked when she gave away her library to the witches' college. Very carefully she laid a tassel of cobweb over wounded Wind Cat and said some words.

Meanwhile her niece, too furious
for good manners, flew across the road
to where Mr Blyde was busy cutting his
front grass border with a Hover-Mow.

'Your horrible *beast* of a dog has nearly killed your poor cat!' Lukey stormed at Mr Blyde. 'You don't deserve to have a cat at all! And that dog ought to be sent to prison!'

'You just mind your own business, young lady!' snapped Mr Blyde, very angry indeed. 'Anyway, you've no call to say Tinker did it. Much more likely it was a fox from the woods.'

'I saw the dog, barking and carrying on outside our gate. If your cat dies, it will be his fault.'

'If you don't go back home this minute, my girl, you're going to get the rough side of my tongue. And I'll have a word to say to your auntie. That's no way to address an adult. Run along now, I'm in a hurry to get this done, we're off to Bournemouth this afternoon.'

'I wish you'd stay in Bournemouth for *ever*!' shouted Lukey, crying, and she ran home. After lunch Mrs Blyde came round with tins of dried milk and Pussymix.

'We're ever so obliged to you for taking care of poor Tibbles while we're away,' she said hurriedly. 'And, of course, if there should be a vet's bill, we'll be glad to pay it.'

'I should think so, the pigs,' muttered Lukey as the big shiny fawn-coloured car purred off into the woods.

Whether due to Aunt Mildrith's clever nursing, or because he had not yet used up all his nine lives, the wounded cat recovered before his owners returned from Bournemouth. For six days Aunt Mildrith had kept a continuous patch of sunshine on the lawn, and

Wind Cat basked in it, limp and dozing on his bit of mat while Lukey squatted beside him, reading bits out of Aunt Mildrith's old black book.

'It's very interesting, Wind Cat, this book,' she told him; and she had an idea that he was listening, as he licked and licked at the terrible gashes that Tinker's teeth had made.

Now and again Lukey would glance
up at the sky and murmur a few words.
Sometimes nothing happened, but
sometimes she would laugh with pleasure
and excitement as a tiny spiral of cloud
whirled round above them and blew a
few yellowing leaves off an apple tree.
Wind Cat sometimes stretched out a
lazy paw and tapped one of the leaves
as it scuffled by.

'Wait a while, Wind Cat!' Lukey
warned him. 'Not just yet! Not until
you are quite better.'

'Oh dear, have you got your head
stuck in that old book again?' sighed
Aunt Mildrith, passing by with a garden
trowel or her sky-watching telescope.
'Don't you think it would be better if
you put it back in the cupboard and
invited a couple of your school friends

to tea?'

But Lukey said that her school friends found two miles from the village too far to walk.

By the time the Blydes came back from Bournemouth, Wind Cat's wounds were healed, and he no longer limped. But now he had discovered how comfortable it was in Aunt Mildrith's kitchen, where he had lain on a blanket in front of her glowing stove while his wounds were at their worst. And he was not at all inclined to return to Bide-a-Wee. In fact he simply refused to go. Time after time Aunt Mildrith picked him up and carried him round. Before she was back at her frontdoor, Wind Cat would be there before her, or through the kitchen window. He made it plain that was where he preferred to live.

Mr Blyde was very annoyed about this. He came round to say so.

'Much obliged to you, of course, for taking care of Tib while we were away – but what's the use of having a cat that's never at home? In my opinion your niece plays with Tib too much. That's the truth of the matter. I'd be obliged if you'd tell her to stop. She ought not to encourage him to come round here. People should not entice away other people's animals.'

He was in the middle of saying all this to Aunt Mildrith, standing very red faced and indignant on her front doorstep, when Wind Cat shot through the open garden gate, closely pursued by the barking, yelling, snapping, slavering Tinker.

Wind Cat dashed round the corner of Aunt Mildrith's house.

Mr Blyde, rather discomposed, made a grab for the dog's collar.

'Now, *Tink*! Now you stop that! Bad boy. Well, as I was saying, Miss Web, I'd be greatly obliged if you'd tell your niece to stop enticing the cat round here,' he told Aunt Mildrith, and he strode off homewards, dragging the agitated and noisy Tinker by his collar.

Just out of sight round the corner of the house, boiling with rage, Lukey held and stroked and soothed Wind Cat, whose heart was thudding like a kettledrum.

'There, there, it's all right now, poor Wind Cat, he's gone, he's gone; and this time he's going to *stay* gone. But you've got to help me, Wind Cat, I can't manage by myself.

Frowning with concentration, Lukey opened Aunt Mildrith's old black book.

After about five minutes the sky had turned as black as burnt toast. The wind rose up and began to howl, making a sound like a chainsaw, wheeeeeoo. A lot of leaves, and some green apples, flew off the apple trees.

Aunt Mildrith, glancing from the kitchen window, observed that the house called Bide-a-Wee began to spin round and round like a chimney-cowl, slowly at first, then so fast that it was just a red, pink and yellow blur. Then house, garage, garden and inhabitants

rose from the ground, still spinning, and
vanished from view. Nothing remained
on the opposite side of the crossroads
but a bald patch of ground.

'Mysterious Appearance of house in Laburnum Road,' said the headline in the *Bournemouth Weekly Chronicle*.

'Bournemouth residents were startled last Friday to find that a complete house had apparently been erected overnight on an empty plot of land where the Sunnyside Infants' School had recently been demolished. The Housing Department says that no application for Planning Permission had been made or granted.'

Aunt Mildrith, reading this paragraph in the paper, sighed, and looked out of the window to where Lukey and Wind Cat were chasing one another in and out of swiftly moving patches of sunshine. An autumn gale had been blowing all day. By now the patch of ground where Bide-a-Wee had stood was covered with fallen beech leaves from the woods.

Oh well, thought Aunt Mildrith, I did my best not to influence the child. But the habit is in the family and I suppose it was bound to come out sooner or later. And I daresay she will be able to make a living as well that way as any other.

Taking her camera from the kitchen dresser, Aunt Mildrith strolled out on to the lawn, looked up, focused the lens on the windy sky, and took some pictures of an extremely interesting set of dinosaur prints which went clear across the middle from one horizon to the other.

SEA MICE

ONCE THERE WAS A GIRL CALLED Hella who lived in a small wooden house on a cold northern coast. Each night in winter she could look out of her bedroom window and see the Northern Lights flashing in the sky. They looked like the fingers of a giant hand, beckoning red and green above the black sea.

Hella had a plum tree that was all her own. Her father, a sea captain, had planted it for her on the day she was born, at the top of the sandy cliff where their house was built. The tree grew faster than Hella, and spread its branches wide, but bore no fruit until her seventh birthday, when it produced one tiny plum, clear as glass.

'You must not pick the fruit yet,' said Hella's father. 'The tree must be allowed to keep its fruit, for it is not a common tree but came from a temple in the land of Zipanou. When you and the tree are both twelve years old, then you can pick the plums.'

After that, Hella's father had to call his crew together, and they embarked in his ship *Elda* and sailed away, far away to the north, to the distant point where sea and sky meet together. On, on, out of sight they sailed, and never came back.

'Poor souls, they have been lost at sea,' people in the nearest town said. And about the ship, *Elda*, Hella heard them say, 'The deadly sea mice got her.'

Hella wondered many times to herself what the deadly sea mice might be like. She had never seen them. Fierce little things, she thought they must be, with sharp, sharp needle-sharp teeth, hungry little swimming mice who gnawed and chewed away at the planks of ships until they broke to pieces and sank under the waves.

Hella pondered and pondered about the sea mice, as she wandered along the shore. While, in the silent house, her mother, instead of cleaning the rooms or weeding the garden, sat still with sorrowful heart and idle hands, grieving for her husband.

One night Hella had a strange dream and woke up crying: 'Oh, mother! I saw the sea mice! I saw the sea mice coming with their sharp teeth to eat up you and me as they ate up my father and his ship!'

But her mother said slowly, 'No, no, child. There are no such things as sea mice. What sank your father's ship was the *seam ice* – the thin skin of ice that forms between two icebergs, which breaks, and melts, and forms again, and sometimes traps a ship in its jaws.'

Despite what her mother had said, for many months after that, and even years, Hella went on dreaming and wondering about the sea mice; only now she did not think of them as savage and wicked, but just wild and lively and carefree, scampering on their own concerns over the frozen ocean.

Every year, at fruit time, Hella longed to pick the plums from her tree. There was never a large crop, not more than five or six fruit each year, but they were very fine, clear all through, like glass, so that the plum-stones in the middle could be seen, pale greenish-amber in colour.

Each year the plums ripened, and fell off the tree, and rolled down the sandy cliff into the sea.

When Hella was nine, her mother

pined away and died of grieving, and there were no other relations to look after the child. Hella was left alone, with nothing in the world but her plum tree.

'Remember child, remember not to pick the plums until you are twelve years old,' her mother reminded Hella just before she died. 'Your father brought the seed from a temple in Zipanou, and the priest told him that bad luck would fall upon anybody who touched the fruit before the tree's twelfth summer. When you and the tree are twelve, child, then you may pick the fruit and it will bring you luck.'

After her mother's death, Hella was obliged to leave the little wooden house, and go away to look for work.

She walked twenty miles to the town, and found a place as kitchenmaid in a big house. Her mistress was a hard woman, and Hella was kept busy all day long, sweeping, dusting, carrying pails of water, lighting fires, peeling potatoes, washing clothes. All day long she had to  work so hard that, when night came, she fell asleep as soon as she lay down on her hard, cold bed. Then she began to dream.

Every night she dreamed about the sea. In her sleep she thought that she could still hear the sound of the waves –

although the coast was twenty long miles away. And Hella dreamed about the sea mice, frisking through the foam at the water's edge, and scampering on the sandy shore. Now they seemed kind little creatures, friendly and welcoming.

'Don't grieve, Hella!' they said. 'We will help you by and by. Wait patiently.'

Hella was allowed only one day's holiday a year. But at least she might choose at what season the day fell, and so she chose her birthday, which fell in August, when the evenings are still long and light, and the plums are ripe.

On her first holiday Hella jumped out of bed just after midnight, put on her clothes, let herself out of the house, and set off to walk to the sea coast, to the cliff where her father's house had stood and where her plum tree grew.

The walk was long and tiring. By the time she reached the cliff, the sun shone high in the sky, and she felt sad to see how shabby and uncared for the little wooden house had become. Nobody lived there any longer. Weeds grew in the garden, and the gate hung on one hinge.

But Hella's plum tree was thriving. It had grown big and healthy, stretching its branches up and out in the shape of a fan. They were covered with a fine crop of fruit, plums big as gulls' eggs and clear as crystal, each with a pale yellow stone at its heart. The plums flashed in the rays of the climbing sun as Hella walked along the sandy beach below the cliff. She longed to pick the plums – even just one! – but knew that she must not for another two years.

When she was just below the tree
on the clifftop, a large bird floated over-
head; all grey and white it was, and cast
a black shadow on the wet sand. As
Hella gazed up at it, shading her eyes
and smiling in wonder, for she had
never seen such a large bird before, an
arrow flew from the clifftop and pierced
its heart.

The bird fell dead on the beach,
and from above Hella heard a shout of
triumph.

Down from the cliff ran a red-haired
boy. He was big, and rather fat, and carried a bag of arrows slung over his
shoulder. In his hand he held an
unstrung bow. Taking no notice of
Hella, he pulled three feathers from the
bird's tail and stuck them into his head-
band.

'Oh, why did you shoot the beautiful bird, why did you do such a thing?'
she cried.

He glanced at her scornfully.

'What affair is it of yours?' he said.
'That was not *your* bird !'

And without
another word he
climbed back to
the top of the cliff
and shook the
boughs of the
plum tree until all
the fruit fell off.
He did not eat the
plums, or pocket
them, but kicked

them idly down the cliff, and, with a
careless jerk of his wrist, flung three or
four of them into the sea.

'Why, why did you do that?' cried
Hella again.

'It's not *your* tree,' sneered the boy.
'It belonged to an old fellow who, they
say, was eaten by the sea mice. Sea
mice! As if anybody believed in *them*!'
And he said again, 'It's not your tree,'
before turning to stride away, whistling,
along the cliffs.

No, thought Hella, it is not my tree
now, but it will be in two years' time.

She looked sadly down at the body
of the beautiful bird, which lay on the
sand where the boy had left it, though
the tide was creeping closer. Then Hella
saw that thousands of tiny white mice
had come crowding out of the surf and
were taking hold of the feathered body
with their strong little paws. They
pulled and tugged the bird into the

waves until it vanished from view. At this sight, Hella felt a little comforted. They will take care of the bird, she thought.

Next the mice scampered on to the sand in order to tidy up the spot where the bird had lain, washing away the blood, making all clean and smooth as it had been before. They took not the slightest notice of Hella, but ran to and fro about her ankles, faster than drops of sea water or grains of sand blowing in the wind.

The sea mice were just the way she had dreamed them, no bigger than acorns, white, and frosted all over with salt, so that their ears and whiskers and the tassels on their tails twinkled like grains of diamond in the rays of the sinking sun. And so did their eyes.

Sea Mice

Now Hella knew that she must leave the beach and walk all the long tiring way back to the town where her mistress lived. 'Goodbye, sea mice!' she called. 'Take care of my plum tree. I will see you next year.' The sea mice made no reply but went busily on with what they were doing.

Another year passed. Hella was kept hard at work, sweeping, dusting, scrubbing, fetching and carrying. Sometimes she was scolded, sometimes she was beaten. Always she had very little to eat. And every night, on her hard bed, she dreamed about the sea mice, darting about on the sand or frisking in the shallows of the sea.

When Hella's next holiday came she rose, as before, just after midnight, and set off to walk the twenty miles to the beach. From far away, this year, she could see in the rising sun how big and handsome her plum tree had grown. But the little wooden house was now hardly more than a pile of rotting boards.

As Hella walked to the top of the cliff and paused to admire the heavy crop of plums that grew on her tree, she heard a thud of hoofs behind her, and turned in time to see a great stag come plunging up the landward side of the cliff.

In pursuit of the stag rode a red-haired huntsman on a black horse, and two black dogs ran ahead of the horse, baying and yelping. Just as the stag reached the clifftop the huntsman loosed an arrow, which sang through the air and struck it in the neck.

The stag gave a loud bellow of pain and sprang out from the clifftop, landing at the sea's edge on the shore below. It was badly hurt and bleeding, Hella could see – drops of blood splashed down on the white sand – but it staggered into the waves, and plunged through the surf, and managed to swim away, out into deep water.

The huntsman cursed long and furiously when he saw his quarry escape him. Leaping off his horse, he beat the two dogs, who howled and whimpered. Then, casting an angry glance at Hella, the hunter strode to the plum tree, which he shook and shook until all the fruit fell off. A few plums he crammed into his pockets, the rest he kicked into the sea below.

'Well, don't look at me so sour-faced!' he growled at Hella. 'It isn't *your* tree!'

And he remounted his horse and galloped away, followed by the two dogs.

No, thought Hella, it is not my tree now; but next year it will be.

After the hunter had gone she walked down to the beach and watched

the little sea mice come out of the
creamy surf to clean away the drops of
blood left by the stag as it
limped over the sand. The
mice rubbed against Hella's ankles and
sometimes scampered right over her
feet; she thought they looked at her
with friendship in their tiny
dazzling eyes.

And then she was obliged to turn
away from the sea and walk all the long
road back to the town.

Another year of hard work and
harsh words passed.

Once more it was time for Hella's
free day. She rose just after the town
clock had struck midnight, dressed
herself, and walked to the shore,
arriving at sunrise, for she was older
now, and could walk faster.

This year, she thought, I am allowed to pick my plums.

But when she came to the top of the cliff she was dismayed to hear the sound of angry shouts and the clang of weapons. Looking down on the beach below she saw two men fighting savagely: one had red hair, the other black. They fought with swords and daggers, thrusting and slashing. The white sand was kicked and trampled all over with their footprints, and splashes of blood lay where they had wounded one another. In early sunshine their shadows raced behind them, long and black and sharp. Above them hung the plum tree, heavy with its crop of glittering fruit.

'Oh, stop!' cried Hella. 'Oh, please stop! Oh, why are you fighting?'

But they took no notice of her

words. Both were bleeding from many cuts; by now the sand was scarred and stained red as if the beach, too, were bleeding. At last, when they had fought for more than two hours, the red-headed man, who was the taller of the two, managed to pierce his enemy right through the heart. But as the other dropped dead, he too, tottered and fell to his knees, and then over on to his side.

A moment later there were two dead men lying on the shore.

No more than a single moment after that, thousands of little sea mice came dashing out of the surf, and they set to work without wasting a moment, dragging the two dead bodies into the waves, cleaning up the scuffed and bloodstained sand, smoothing and washing where it had been trampled and soiled, until all was clear and flat and white once more.

Hella, sitting on a rock, watched the mice, and it seemed to her that they gave her friendly glances. When they had done, and the beach was empty and clean, Hella climbed to the top of the cliff where her plum tree grew. The branches were heavy with fruit. Every glassy plum had a rose-coloured stone at its heart. Taking hold of the boughs, Hella shook them vigorously, until all the plums had fallen off and rolled down to the beach below. From where she stood, the shore looked as if it were covered with diamonds and rubies. 'Sea mice! Sea mice!' Hella called. 'My plums are for you!' And the sea mice looked up at her with eyes that sparkled as brightly as the fallen plums. Then Hella ran down the cliff again, and she ran towards the sea.

Observing her do this, the sea mice, frisking in the lacy surf, pulled back a huge wing of green sea-water, as the corner of a quilt is pulled back on a bed, making a dry path for Hella to walk out into the deep ocean.

With bare dry feet she walked away from the shore, far, far into the distance,

following the track taken by the hurt
stag, and by her father's ship. Close
behind her followed a procession of sea
mice, each carrying a rosy-hearted
plum. And, behind the sea mice, the
water closed together again.

Five minutes later, nobody would have been able to guess what had happened.

Next autumn the leaves blew off Hella's plum tree. During the winter a landslide carried away the cliff top, and the ruined house. Hella's tree, roots and all, slid into the waves and floated away, who knows where? Perhaps to the land of Zipanou.